MARRIED TO THE SKY

KADAMBARI GUPTA

Contents

1

Married to the sky

Marriage a topic that was discussed or brought about time and again,

At any party or festive gathering either directly or indirectly taunts were sensed around her marriage,

But varsha had a plan where marriage was miles away from life she dreamt of living ,

She aspired to be a pilot and fly in the sky focused on this goal would stay away from these discussions,

As ,much as possible her mother would tell her no ,matter how much you,

Try such discussions and questions are unavoidable and with that statement,

Time took a giant leap and she completed her training as a pilot and then,

Got ready for her first flight as she flew for the first time from Mumbai to goa

Being miles above from the earth was an experience beyond words and then,

Flew many flights subsequently whenever at the airport newly married ,

Couples would be seen her face would just brighten like the stars in the sky,

Her eyes being wide open would dream of getting married and then roam,

Around holding each others hands like those couples one day,

She would make notes in her diary what are the qualities her future husband,

Shall have intelligent good looking supportive understanding well established,

In his career and field . her mother was worried about finding a good ,match,

For there daughter so they decided to make her account on a ,matrimonial website,

And uploaded her best pictures on the site as that would attract good match,

Many boys viewed her profile and expressed there desire to meet her ,

She would meet and they would ask her about her interests and future plans,

Meeting would go well but then they would reject the proposal this went,

On for several years and whenever any photo or proposal would be rejected,

By her then it would be taken as commission of a serious crime how could you reject him,

He was such a good looking boy well settled and earning seven figures why don't you understand,

What we go through as everyone asks why aren't u getting her married how can she remain,

Unmarried up till now that day couldn't take it anymore packed the suitcase and ran away,

My father gave the keys of the other two bedroom hall kitchen house that he had purchased,

Long back but did not tell anyone about it and it was a well furnished house so started living,

There and continued to fly and then the night when one returned back home was dead tired,

As it was an international flight so just crashed into the bed next morning it was a holiday,

So was in the balcony just sitting and looking at the beautiful view then saw the sky that is,

Vast and its length can't be measured how magnificent it ,looks the color blue and white.

Is close to the uniform one wears and just kept looking at the sky now every Sunday would,

Go and start gazing at the sky and then realized yes have fallen in love "oh my god" really,

Began to tickle myself to believe that yes love is in the air and in this room this sky is the,

Love that fills the void that is felt in this life,

Would go for dates at rooftop cafes have coffee and sandwiches looking at the sky.

And just feel like a teenager who would wait for the English teacher to come and start the class,

In his sweet voice would explain the chapters and then would ask any doubts and girls would be like,

"oh my god " sir we have doubts will discuss it with you in the next class its beautiful to experience,

Those feelings once again and that day it started raining and got drenched as rains was desired by ,

This heart since a very long time and asked the sky I want rain I want rain not feeling good at all,

Rains will cheer this soul up and then rains weren't expected but clouds started showering there,

Water and I started to collect these drops in these hands but they would flow down from the hands,

How romantic is the sky and just like wives expect gifts from husbands on birthdays and anniversary,

Similarly all demands of ,mine are made to the sky and then on valentines day purchased a bunch,

Of red and white roses and then sat down on one knee and proposed to the sky,

Dear sky I have fallen for you deeply the love is unconditional weaved with emotions this,

World wont understand will you marry me and sky through lightening and thunder said yes,

Next day purchased a red saree and made a garland out of flowers at home and from the,

Balcony threw garland at the sky and as one was applying vermillion the wind blew fast and,

Soon the vermillion was all over the face as if sky had applied and then marriage was complete,

Had a good feast and was about to click some pictures that got a call from dad asking how his princess was,

And I said fine and doing well on being asked have I found someone to get married to then told him,

Yes dad found someone and got married today as well dad said wow beta congratulations who is her,

What he does and you didn't tell anyone not even your father why so and told him dad this no one,

Would understand this love story and told him got married to the sky he was shocked and then ,

Explained everything and he being the sweetest dad any daughter could ever ask for said,

Beta you are happy and in the most joyful voice yes dad and then he said fine that's all one wanted,

And then he put the phone down.

Then continued to flying and each day would be so exciting as one would meet my husband,

Who was waiting for his wife to sit in the aircraft and then exchange pleasantries in the sky.

As the aircraft flew high in the sky.

My mother was flabbergasted on hearing what her daughter did and her dialogue,

"what have you done what will people think" she needs help as how can anyone,

Get married to the sky it's an unacceptable decision people get married to a person,

A human being and not to the sky what will happen in the future god only knows,

When her friends will get married and being a witness to the ceremonies being,

Performed this face will be wet with tears as to why this isn't happening with me,

I shall have a husband too well it was a mothers concern and worry for her daughter,

That spoke and one had to hear it and then before leaving she said is this your final decision,

Think once again who gets married to a sky and then I replied its final no change,

Got married to the sky was warned not to come back here again smiled and bid the family,

Goodbye and came back and then the routine began of flying and coming back lived a blissful,

Life and travel many places meet my soulmate each time the flight would take off the sky,

Would change colors turn white as if its sending rays of peace and love towards his wife

Towards his wife.

2
With the End

She was a medical professor and taught in a reputed college in Jaipur with,

An experience of more than ten years her teaching methods were different from.

Other professors and that made her favorite among the students the lectures she took.

Always saw full attendance the classroom would be fully occupied that at times,

Students had to sit on the floor and attend the class.

It was an off day she slept late last night woke up saw many missed calls,

The calls were from an old school friend with whom the connection was lost,

As she had changed school after tenth to pursue science they ,made a plan,

To meet at the coffee shop it was a bright sunny afternoon and they saw each other,

Came running close and clasped each other tightly in there arms the emotions,

Could be seen in those eyes that changed color soon they ordered coffee and

Began there long pending conversation about how life has changed over the years,

And was enthralled to know that her friend has become a writer and has been doing,

Really well and is currently working with a well-known publication house and has,

Many awards as a writer to her credit , and is also a singer and performs in wedding functions only,

On returning back home she pondered over the meeting and realized that growing up there were ,

Stories that were there in the mind box and that wanted to come out on pen and paper but,

Family was against this passion as they felt medicine is a profession of highest standard and,

Rest is just hobby to be pursued to overcome boredom,

Soon the classes in the college were over as preparatory leave for students had begun and ,

Then her friend called and said hey there is a competition for story writing and there is no age limit,

Genre is open why don't you participate sending the details on Whatsapp replied smartphone isn't working ,

The bestie in her beautiful sweet voice said don't worry you send your email-id will mail the details,

There and this opportunity has come make use of it don't let it go soon received the mail and,

Registered for the competition and then began to write a story about a girl who loved to swim and,

Would go to the club every Sunday one day while swimming her leg got collided with an object ,

And went underwater to find it and was shocked to see a leather bag in the pool what that bag contained,

Her ,mind began to wonder soon the bag was handed over to the instructor who was there to teach all,

Amateur swimmers and then finally the bag was opened and it had so many wrist watches and chains,

That they started falling out from the bag everyone was shocked to see this soon the head of the club,

Was informed and they started investigating this matter soon after thorough investigation it was revealed,

That this bag belonged to a student who was refused to be taught by the instructor because of his behavior,

Towards other students he would insult them and throw away there swimming goggles in the pool that day.

Was about to push a boy who was about to go into the pool through the stairs and not just dive in ,

They found that the bag belonged to him as his cousin brother who was taking tennis coaching at the,

Same club confirmed that this bag was gifted to him by his parents as a birthday gift and the keychain had,

His name engraved on it ,many students who had complained to the instructor about there watches and,

Chains being stolen finally could recover them now search began for this thief they informed his parents and,

The police and soon search began for him and it was found out that he has committed suicide by jumping from ,

His terrace building as the servant informed the parents that he said want to play on the terrace today and saw,

Him going up and then heard a scream and came only to see that he was lying down in the pool of blood,

But his body was not found as the police reached the residence they searched everywhere dug the garden ,

Went to the servant quarters the body was not found it was a mystery where was the body how he committed ,

This theft when did he threw the bag in the pool and why he could have sold those watches and chains run away,

With the money where was his body did he committed this theft alone or there were people along with him,

All members and visitors of the club were thoroughly questioned and the entire area was sealed but found no clues,

As if everything was erased at the residence not even a single particle of evidence could be found,

No stains of blood was found on the floor all passers by and vendors were questioned,

Including the watchman but no one saw him lying down did the servant knew anything about it , in the house his room all the things

Were perfectly arranged nothing was missing there were many questions this case raised after months of investigation the

Case was closed the pool and club began to function she went for swimming again to find again there was an object that

Collided with her feet now what was that and why did it collided again only with her feet only with her feet.

3

The Sugar Paranthas

Sugar paratha is not just a food item for this being its an emotion that one carries,

Was craving for sugar paratha for weeks and on Sunday requested mamma to make,

Sugar paratha for her darling daughter with not only sugar ghee and wheat flour,

But also warmth love and compassion these ingredients make paratha a delight,

Mom made it and the moment took the first bite oh god it was heaven really ,

Just after finishing three sugar parathas went and kissed my dear mother and,

She smiled and said so elated to see that you liked the parathas so ,much,

Next day at office was a very hectic day as there were meetings one after the other,

and no time for lunch or even have a cup of tea or coffee finally the meeting,

Got over and then it was lunch time breathed a sigh of relief as finally a break for lunch

and my stomach it was growling like anything as one was given punishment for starvation

by someone.

As I opened the foil wow baby it was sugar parathas and each one asked,

For one bite so she had given six parathas I got only one and rest were taken,

Away by all dear friends and the moment they had there first bite god they were,

Speechless they said god they are so tasty and delicious we never had sugar parathas,

In our life as only aloo parathas with curd was ,made for Sunday breakfast but this gosh,

It tastes divine and they blessed mom a thousand times and even asked when would bring,

Sugar parathas again for lunch.

Next day there was a call that in the office all systems are down due to a power cut and,

There is some internal problem in the wiring so work and calls shall be done from home,

Until further notice so would have calls and ,meeting on zoom and on Sunday everyone joined,

Together and said when will we get to have sugar parathas and with a smile replied soon friends,

Just wait for office to resume our boss MR Ghosh came on call and said well how have all you been,

Dear team and second family for me back after a vacation and got to know from our clients that,

The team and employees in the company are very efficient and hardworking in your absence they,

Handled everything quite well all queries were cleared and prompt response was given for all ,

Questions that were asked and felt great indeed gratitude to each and every member of this team,

Who worked relentlessly and gave this company not only hundred but two hundred percent and,

Anshika been hearing a lot about your mothers recipe of sugar parathas and would like to try them too,

Saw all pictures with paratha in hand on the group and they looked really delicious so would like to try,

Them too.

Hearing those words mom literally jumped with joy and said all your office colleagues including,

MR Ghosh will be treated with sugar parathas made by this skilled chef and after a week received,

A e-mail regarding wiring work being over and resuming office from 15th of September and mom,

Made the parathas and kept it in the lunch box and went for her yoga class ,

At the office when it was lunch time everyone was excited to eat sugar parathas and the moment,

One opened the tiffin there were no parathas was shocked and felt embarrassed in front of all,

Colleagues and MR Ghosh but decided to compensate by ordering pizza for everyone from Zomato they ,

Relished the pizzas and the butterscotch mousse cake and then came back home in a foul mood,

Mom asked what happened and told her and she was as shocked as I was ,

She said that before leaving for yoga class parathas were packed in the foil and put it in the lunch box,

Along with pickles and napkins so where did it go who took away all parathas are thieves these days,

Stealing food as well from other people homes along with cash electronic items and jewels ,

Then on Sunday asked mom to make besan halwa for me and she made it and kept it on the table,

I came after a shower only to see the bowl empty and only some crumbs of halwa left to eat,

Again was perplexed where is the food going from the house suddenly heard some noises and,

Then went outside following the noise and saw a group of monkeys were eating the halwa in there,

Own wooden bowl and then realized may be those sugar parathas were eaten by them that day,

Decided to shoo the monkeys away as they will come each day and take away food from our house ,

But then a thought that crossed made this girl filled with anger to come back home the thought was,

We as humans have money to buy food and other eatables from the market and even water we purchase,

From the store but what about these animals they cant speak and work earn money they too have families,

Just like ours to feed and take care of like humans go in the morning to search for work and jobs they too ,

Leave in the morning to go and search for food so from that day onwards would take some food and keep,

It near the tree on which they stayed so that they don't come inside the house and take away the food.

4

He made an Instrument

Music was his life ever since radio had entered in his house would listen FM each day and would request

Romantic melodies each day and would hum these songs along with the artist whose song was played

And from then his interest in ,music began and would do riyaaz religiously every day and one day decided

To audition for school choir and music teacher was impressed by his voice and included him in school choir

Every time when special assembly would be held and choir would perform his voice would touch the hearts

Of all students teachers and the principal . one day it was a Sunday afternoon and he was singing as usual

Suddenly his father arrived and saw dear son singing and got extremely agitated and flabbergasted at him

Threw the radio away and warned him not to sing in the future and his mother came and asked what happened

And he said your darling son was singing why he should be studying just talked to a friend and his son has said

Dad I want to pursue civil services in the future and then asked about my son was so ashamed to say

That he has still not figured about his ambition the son couldn't bear any more insults and torture and went

To his room crying he was a devotee of Lord Ganesha and would vent all pain and agony in front of him

Next day before leaving for school was called by his father and received a strict warning not to sing at all

And leave the school choir saying you cant manage studies and school together its ninth standard you need time,

Went to school it was ,music class and there teacher announced that he was been selected to perform as a solo artist,

For a competition that is going to be held next month the teacher was surprised to see that rather than being excited,

He got scared and shaken up by this news on being asked what was the reason hugged MR Das tightly and told him,

Everything MR Das said relax son will come to your house this weekend and talk to your dad and figure something out

And the bell rang ,music class was over on Sunday ,MR Das came to his residence tried his level best convince him to,

Let there son participate in the competition he even said that the entry fee shall be paid by him just give the permission,

It's a big opportunity but he remained adamant and in a bitter baritone told MR Das to leave there residence with immediate

Effect and never show this face ever again and that night made him write an application to leave the choir forever using coercion,

And undue influence also used the most powerful tool of mother swear that you wont sing in the choir he was hassled and depressed as if life has come to an end so brutal for him,

To the core and then next day when his friends asked him reason behind leaving the choir cited studies and, preparation,

MR Das was disappointed but promised himself that he would participate in the competition so he called him in the next free period,

And recorded his voice and sent it for the competition since the entries for the competition were so many that it took a long time,

For the judges to finalize the result till then annual exams approached cleared the exams with good , marks and showed the report card

To his father had full hope that now dad will not remain angry with me anymore as stood second in the class but dad said

"what are you showing this this only ninety two percent marks" my friends son test scored ninety nine point nine percent and

Stood first in the class felt dejected and left the room his mother came and consoled him said beta lets go out and eat your,

Favorite cheese pizza and cold coffee he said okay break from hell and he went to a newly opened place called

Love for Pizza and came back with a cheerful smile soon the results of the competition came in which he stood first,

All over India and his photo was printed in the newspaper and all his friends came to his place to congratulate him and,

Soon his dad came to know and in a fit of rage the next day before the new session began made him appear for a test,

And got admission in a boarding school miles away from the city he was crying inconsolably and requested his father,

Not to sent him there but to no avail soon they reached the boarding school and that night had his long pending,

Conversation with Lord Ganesh and asked him why me what wrong had I done such harsh punishment one received,

And slept next day was Sunday and met his roommate Keshin and soon both of them got along and then keshin,

Discovered Lokesh passion for singing and asked him and his face was red in color he offered an ice cream Belgian chocolate,

That happened to be his favorite and he narrated the entire story and his eyes turned wet how could a father be so cruel and,

Harsh but made sure that here his singing wont be interrupted soon the session began both became best friends and then,

Would spend a lot of time together one day went around the campus and found an old garage went ahead and found it was open.

Inside the garage there was dark and keshin opened his brand new i-phone gifted by dear dad and then they saw so a broken .

Guitar and a table there Lokesh decide to pick them and make something out of it and then keshin him soon they reached there

Hostel and hide those instruments under the trunk after the terminal exams were over he began ,making an instrument out of the,

Broken guitar by cutting the strings and attaching threads and wooden blocks soon an instrument was ready and he played and

A sweet baritone was released at night when keshin would be asleep he began to write lyrics for the first ever original song.

And within a few weeks his song was ready and final exams of class tenth was over chose commerce along with keshin and then,

Keshin shot his song on the i-phone and released it on youtube audience were amazed to see the new instrument he ,made out,

Of a broken guitar his mother who hardly would eat and sleep after her dear son was sent to a boarding school because of being a

Great singer was happy to see the song her son had written titled "why this punishment " and soon the school came to know about it,

But the Principal supported his talent and said don't worry about your father just focus on studies and singing and soon he was invited,

By clubs nearby for shows and concerts he even taught ,music in the school to all students of junior classes after twelfth for the next step towards his career was admissions in university so decided to apply in all,

The colleges nearby and decided not to go back home and stay here his mother one day came to meet and when he saw her came,

Running and gave her a tight hug and said mom missed you and her silence was the answer that she reciprocated the same

He said ,mom lets go and meet keshin my friend and she said let him come was perplexed and soon it was his dad who came along

With folded hands said sorry sorry beta a thousand times and told the story of how he had the passion for dancing and wanted to,

Be a dancer but then everyone would ridicule his father by saying what ,kind of a profession is this dance instructor why he cant be,

A teacher or in the government service and often he would be beaten up by his grandfather each time the word dance was uttered,

His friends son who said will appear for civil services failed in class twelfth and is now preparing for compartment exam in fact he made me,

Understand what trauma and torture one had put you through instead of being proud of your achievements always criticized your talent,

Pls forgive me son Lokesh just came and hugged his dad and even sang the song he had written for his father with the tunes being played,

On the instrument he made and after the song was over the instrument broke into pieces they were shocked but keshin was relaxed and calm,

Lokesh asked keshin why are u so calm and he replied the purpose of this instrument was over so it broke the instrument was meant to,

Play tunes that unites two hearts of a father and son and when that purpose was accomplished the instrument broke,

After that all went to the hostel to pack there stuff and leave for there hometowns and begin there undergraduate studies and music journey.

5

The newspaper man

The Newspaper man always had its time set to deliver newspapers at our homes,

In the ,morning each day at about seven o clock he would come on his cycle,

And would sing a song upon his arrival that would be like,

Its morning time read the paper read the paper there is a piece of news

That needs your attention that needs your attention,

With these two lines he would deliver the newspapers in all the apartments of.

Our building always optimistic and positive about life his smile would,

Erase ones sadness as would offer help to anyone in the building without having

Any motive or purpose behind .

ঢ়ঢ়ঢ়

that day as he was delivering the newspapers he saw a bunch of people that,

Were roaming around and taking rounds of the building they looked suspicious to.

Him and asked them yes sir any assistance you want and they said no and'.

Then further questioning began never saw you here before and then they replied.

Yes we are looking for affordable house three bedroom hall kitchen and a colony.

Well guarded and safe for children so our estate agent suggested this colony a.

Perfect residential area and we came here to see a house here replied okay and.

Went ahead with his work and then one day he got a shock of his life something.

He had never thought that would happen the residents of the colony had.

Complained to the secretary about him bringing drugs wrapped in newspapers.

To distribute it amongst the children on being questioned his reaction was.

Never even in the wildest dreams can I ever think about doing such a crime,

Iam innocent they checked the newspaper bag and even the quarter and what,

They found was shocking there were several packets of drugs that were found and.

On getting it tested by experts they were cocaine and heroine one of the most.

Hazardous drugs they also found some notes under the ,mattress which made it.

Believable putting all factors together that he was selling drugs to the children.

Of the colony and would bring him inside the gate by hiding them under his bag.

Of newspapers one of the residents in the colony got so agitated that he bought,

His sons cricket bat and beat him black and blue and even made a complaint to,

The publication and since the offence was serious was suspended from his job.,

Until further notice the newspaper man Hansan came back home howled and cried,,

Was feeling helpless that how these drugs came in his bag and how to prove his innocence.

ᗑᗑᗑ

The next day Benika came back after completing her doctorate from Lucknow University,

And was looking for Hansan whom she used to address as "bhaiya " to give him the news,

That now she will be called DR Benika was just taking a small tour of the neighborhood,

Was surprise to see the bunch of people also doing the same thing and asked them,

Never saw you here before and they replied oh we were looking for a house there and,

The Real Estate Agent said this colony is the best rated under top category for affordable,

Housing and safety especially for women and children when she reached home and asked,

About Hansan Bhaiya her mother narrated the whole incident what really I cant believe this,

Were her words and she ran away to the quarters where Hansan Bhaiya stayed and knocked the,

Door and no one opened soon pushed the door and it was open saw Hansan Bhaiya lying on the,

Floor and some pieces of rotten chapattis scattered on the floor and broken pieces of glass worried,

What might have happened she called her family doctor immediately whose clinic was nearby and,

He came and checked him a glucose drip was given and then soon he opened his eyes and saw Benika,

And said beti and she responded yes bhaiya and both began to cry he said iam innocent and not guilty,

Of the crime being accused off and she said I know and will find the real culprit soon and then got his,

x-ray done he had multiple fractures on his spine and legs that were now plastered medicine was given,

and next day she set to find the real culprits suddenly saw a group of boys taking a stroll around the colony,

on being asked they repeated the same story replied ok and went ahead in the garden saw many bottles,

of alcohol drugs and injections called the security guard and the colony kids and all were stunned to se this,

asked them what are these packets doing here and injections and all were clueless then another boy came, and,

replied some people in the night when he was awake to study saw some men drinking and consuming drugs,

and then the whole story was clear in her mind went on and checked the cctv which was broken however, there,

was another camera that was being installed and was covered by a huge tree with the help of guard and, secretary,

of the building they got that camera and saw the footage where they those group of people that were being, seen,

were actually drug peddlers and they hid those drugs in Hansan Bhaiyas bag to prove him guilty and the, injections,

of morphine belonged to one of the ,members who was an addict himself soon police and drug department was,

informed also some drugs were sold as free samples to teenagers of the building and doctors was informed, who,

did there blood test and found traces of cocaine in there blood however since the habit was not very old it. could,

be controlled easily and all residents went to Hansan Bhaiyas residence and with there hands folded, apologized to,

him for there actions and how they mistreated him and didn't give any chance to even explain his side of. the story,

Even the security guard was reprimanded as how could be allow strangers to enter inside the building, premises,
and believed there story that they had been told by there friends about this colony.

ᐯᐯᐯ

Drugs are substances that can make a person and his family life a living hell it takes a very long time, for people,
To realize that there child has become an addict of a particular substance also we always believe the truth. that,
Is in front of us at times what is being presented may not be the whole truth and be a false story from, beginning to the end,
Hansan Bhaiya is recovering and all charges have been absolved he has been appointed by another publication,
To deliver newspapers and I have decided to raise awareness about substance abuse through internet so, that all the,
Parents and children are aware about how dangerous this addiction is.

6

Emotions and Wealth

It was a hot sunny day and my sons summer vacations had just begun was feeling,

Very bored as all his friends were either out of station or in summer camp I asked him,

To set up his room and sort out his clothes till the time one could finish the work in hand,

Like an obedient son replied "yes mom" and soon he finished his work and then made an,

Entry into ,my room and was shocked to see so many clothes and other things scattered,

Around the bed and then he said "oh my god "mom it seems ,like you have opened a,

Shop today what are all these things and few seem to be quite dirty as well. I said yes beta,

They are very old things and there are two other boxes would you like to see what's inside,

With an excited face said yes but mom my stomach is growling feeling very hungry well,

I was feeling hungry too and decided too order ,mom and sons favorite tomato pasta garlic,

Bread and French fries with cheese dip soon the order was delivered and then began to gorge,

On the delicious food and then he said ,mom lunch done tummy is full now lets see your stuff,

Cant wait anymore then replied okay son lets go and unpack memories today was perplexed when,

Heard unpack memories must be wondering what has happened to ,mom today how can memories.

Be unpacked we aren't coming back from a long holiday where we will unpack luggage anyways,

We headed straight to our room and he sat on the small stool waiting to see the stuff hidden,

Inside those bags.

Then I began opening the bag with the keys and of course with time the locks were very hard and,

Had plenty of dust bunnies on it despite covering them with old tattered bedsheets finally the lock,

Was opened then began taking out stuff that had the first saree one wore for school farewell the,

Frock my grandmother had stitched for me the polo neck sweater that one wore all winters and,

Many other clothes he was looking excited and said mom you used to wear these clothes and make,

Two braids with ribbon and go to school with a loving tone replied yes beta and what is the other,

Stuff so it was the old wooden piggy bank that papa got it made so I put all the money received in it,

The first diary that I wrote and the pen some old notes the flower his father gave and the teddy bear,

On valentines day oh god still remember that ,moment when he surprised me by landing at my house,

That day on 14th of February with a heart shaped chocolate cake and said happy valentines day love,

The notes made during school and college days there were many scarfs that mom had made from old,

Dupattas and I used to cover the face as in college used to change two buses to reach for the first lecture,

For which would get late by half and hour the doll which was dressed as a bride and that doll one had made,

In the stitching class in school those marbles oh my god sheer nostalgia how time flies away soon as one,

Was reminiscing old days saw his face turning red in anger and irritation said "what is all this scrap you, collected mom"he replied.

Are these things worth keeping many are broken from some end and they are so dirty as if they have, bathed in dust.

Mom you wasted my time showing this are these things worth being kept and treasured for such a long, time really,

I cant believe this what if one of my friends had turned up today and seen this mess they would be thinking, and would,

Call scrap collector scrap collector we aren't poor papa is doing so well earning great money you are so, successful ,mom

Papa can buy you so many gifts still you have kept this teddy bear and flower what for you wasted my time, seriously.
and walked from the room while banging the door the heart could feel the sounds and I just pinched myself. to see

Is it a bad dream or was it real he said these words so harsh negative infectious and poisonous and theni put all those,

Things back and sat on the floor in utter disbelief with much heart and love one showed him these things. the memories,

The emotions that these things carried with them and he just pointed out how old they were as if they were. taken from a museum,

Sat down on the floor in utter disbelief kept asking myself "what happened was it for real or it was a bad dream one saw"

Was about to pack all the things and then his father yes my dear loving husband came back after a long work trip and saw,

This face red and swollen in hurried manner as I was packing all the things touching them one by one as, planned to give these,

Items away he saw those things said my god these things you still have them cant believe this and look at, this teddy bear looks so cute,

But not more than you and this flower even after so many years the flower is still the same and I replied in, a rude tone no its not stop lying,

And then put his laptop bag on the bed and wrapped hands around the waist and asked "love what, happened couldn't bear it anymore just,

Hugged him tightly and burst out in tears and kept crying like anything took out handkerchief and wiped, my tears made ginger tea for me,

And asked what was the reason behind this sadness all of a sudden then told him everything was shocked, that how there son could be so rude,

Insensitive and impolite how could such harsh words that are just like injections of poison are uttered from. his mouth , may be its our too ,much

Love and affection that has spoilt him where is our dear spoilt son gone out for a stroll was the answer let. him come back this behavior wont be.

Tolerated at all I said we need to be calm and be patient if you scold him right now then he will feel oh, mom turned dad against me and.

He wont even listen to us his father realized that yes there is a different approach to be adopted to teach our son value of things .

Soon next morning was super excited to see that daddy is back and now will stay with them for next few, days and planned to go for,

Go-karting and swimming so they went as per there plan .,

I decided to go for a relaxing session at the parlor get manicure and pedicure done the moment reached the, parlor the owner greeted me,

With a smile and so ,much warmth and said its been a while since you came glad to see our old customer, more like a family back relax now,

And take a look at our updated services pamphlet and will make sure that you have a relaxing experience here so looked at the menu and

Sipped on the delicious cardamom tea that was served as a welcome drink while flipping through the pages of there services decided to

Go for manicure pedicure and hair spa as in this summer and rising temperatures really took a toll on these long locks of ,soon the session

Began oh cant explain in words how one felt really so relaxed as the nails were clean polished massaged the, dead skin and dirt on this face was removed making it clean like anything in this world,

Same procedure was repeated on the feet as this was going on the words of my son would echo in these, ears so decided to put headphones on,

As the hair spa began the head massage with oil that smelled absolutely divine the massage on the scalp, and, all stress points just released all the ,

Stress into the air one felt then shampoo and hair mask the moment it ended one was like wow how. beautiful the hair looks thanked the owner,

Received a surprise gift pack from them aww was the word that came through these lips then left to meet, my friends over lunch the moment,

One reached oh my god all of them just came together gave a big hug or rather a group hug and then sat, down to order something as rats were,

Just playing in the stomach and then started conversations about our lives post marriage and motherhood, how things have changed and how,

My dear son has become rude and insensitive as the way he responded when one was showing the memory, box her friend replied they see,

Everything in terms of what is and what is out and not as something which has memories associated with it, until and unless they go through,

The same experience only then they will realize the value of things beyond the price and fashion gave a, nod to what she said and enjoyed a,

Delicious Chinese lunch and coffee ice-cream with them and then came back .

For the next one week was busy as getting a pest control done was pending for long so was getting it done. suddenly saw the phone.

Vibrating and then once they left checked the phone and got to know through the group formed on whatsapp where all mothers of,

My son's class are added and we get all updates the vacations have been cut short by a month and classes. will resume as there half-yearly,

Exams will begin early and then pre-board exams of tenth and twelfth standard so students of other class, will make noise and students,

Will get disturbed was stressed by this news as one had planned a long trip but what to do one had to abide. by the circular and rules of.

The school since his dad had come so he was really enjoying and went for a short trip to Jodhpur and. Mount Abu beautiful holiday and did a,

Lot of shopping as well and hot air balloon ride in Mount Abu was an unforgettable experience.

Finally vacations were over and school began everything was back to normal and suddenly one day he. came and went to his room,

And refused to eat lunch thought he might be tired and upset as vacations were cut short by a month but. then by evening stayed,

Inside the room only and one got worried and then went and started knocking said "what happened beta. ??" all well please open the door,

Open the door my son he didn't called up his dad and tried to break the door was getting stressed and. anxious what happened and then,

His dad arrived broke open the door saw him sitting on the floor with his box and then came to us, and started crying inconsolably,

Iam sorry iam sorry pls forgive me pls forgive me were his words gave water and then rubbing my palms on, the forehead asked,

Son what happened and then he said my friend is leaving the city because his fathers transfer and then, came back and saw all gifts cards,

He ,made and gifted and photos of our pre-school days felt bad of how rude I was to you that day when all, precious memories you had,

Taken out and I said they are scrap what is the value of these things today realize how rude and insensitive one was mamma can't we

Stop him he is the only close friend one first gave food and then explained that son the same emotions are, going on in his heart too,

I know you are upset but he will miss his parents here what will be done then supposing we go leaving our dear son with someone else,

Will that be okay relied no mamma then I understand what are you saying so this Sunday lets plan a. farewell party and give him a gift

A special gift what say he said mamma that's a great idea iam up for it but what gift to buy for him I said make something from your own

Hands that will be a special gift and then decided to make a collage of our photos and a sketch of both best, friends together,

So next Sunday all arrangements were made his favorite chocolate truffle cake. Mushroom and cheese pizza, and yes strawberry shake,

As he entered was surprised by the decorations and then there was a party music dance and games cake cutting and a nice lunch was being prepared exclusively for him,

Finally it was time to say goodbye both friends hugged each other and then our son gave a farewell gift which when he opened became,

Teary eyed and he also gifted his dear friend books and a football as both used to play football together left. with a heavy heart and that,

Day while getting ready to sleep got remined of what my friend had said that children only learn about, certain things when they go through,

The same experience like our son learnt to value things for the memories and emotions associated with it and not to equate it with fashion,

Latest trends, prize tag and profit loss percentage.

7
Social Media is Alive

Marzin was a first year student of history honors at Dehradun University was mocked by his,

Classmates for being a studious student and miles away from being the popular guy on whom every,

Girl of the class had a crush on marzin would often feel bad on being asked this question,

Hey MR studious do you have a girlfriend and then everyone would laugh it off by saying,

Look at him he is always into books plus the spectacles that are a decoration to these eyes that look damn. weird.

Don't they and size of these glasses are as big as an elephants trunk and see the hair "oh my god they are. not just.

Hair they are an oil factory all these jokes would really hurt him a lot but what was an option as if at home, would,

Tell the family about this they would also say why cant you be like them why only you are picked up, amongst all,

The students its all your damn fault really what to do seriously try to mingle with them so he would keep, these,

Events stored in the huge store of his heart ..

Then there was a huge revolution that happened and it was yes the social media platform called Friendsbook where.

Each person could connect with another person instantly by making an account on this platform and all the students,

Joined this platform and soon would often send friend requests to each other he was also asked the next day

Hey are you on friendsbook and then others said you are asking the wrong person what will he do there, share notes "ha ha ha",

Soon exams were held and then there was a shift from school to college happened when as soon as he got. enrolled decided to get,

Himself a makeover and then as soon college would start all girls just stunned to see this handsome boy in, college,

It was the orientation day when all students freshers were welcomed to this college where they would, spend three years

Of there lives and may these three years prove to be a life-changing experience for you all there all girls came up to him and asked,

The most awaited question "hey are you on Facebook and with utmost confidence replied yeah and they, just jumped in excitement,

And soon received so many friend requests from girls of his course and of other courses as well life was, awesome and would,

Post pictures each day about going to college coming back classroom scene all students discussing there Facebook status and,

Number of friends they have yes there is a competition it seems account having most number of friends will be rewarded.

With a huge trophy ,when he would visit the canteen would click pictures even then having a cold drink and samosa,

Somehow being on facebook the attention from studies got diverted as was busy updating his profile and, checking other peoples,

Accounts that would often bunk lectures and didn't complete his notes the readings bundle received from the university,

Was kept in the cupboard as it is then one day his elder brother who was working in Mumbai had come. home after a very long time,

Noticed that his brother is not studying as all the notebooks were blank and the white colored pages of the notebooks was clearly,

Visible when he came back got hold of him and in the room asked "what is going on "you are not paying attention to studies and.

The whole day you are only on facebook uploading pictures even posting pictures of having breakfast in the morning and going to

Sleep at night what about studies history honors is not an easy course one of my friends sister is doing the same course but from

Other college she says bhaiya its very tough and the readings are so bulky and voluminous the text seems like rockets flying way,

Above the head listening to all this Marzin replied she must be an average student and not a topper like me ill said through.

His elder brother replied don't be so overconfident and be careful while using social media this platform has its own pros and cons.

Be careful with whom you are chatting and don't accept all friend requests he said okay okay was least interested in hearing this,

Lecture and went back to sleep next day after college got over met school classmates who were waiting at, the auto stand they went,

Up to him and said ,man you have changed so ,much way to go and he replied bro times change look at my, clothes all branded stuff,

Then they asked what about girlfriend do you have any wait for that day and soon you all will see her and, then invited him to the,

Newly opened lounge for all college students called heartdocks said okay fine and then reached there that night and all began

Taking photos and started posting on Facebook and then one of them started laughing and everyone looked at her she said look at,

This pic Almee has posted with her dog looking awful her face just see so much make up come lets write, comments and give her

Some advice on fashion and make-up and hair look at the hair similar to the pet whom she calls biscuit I cant control ,my laugh,

Oh god biscuit she must be nuts who names there dog biscuit come lets post our comments and they asked Marzin to join them as well,

He was reluctant but they oh come on stop being the good boy its fun and one gave in as didn't want to be a, joke once again and on her,

Picture posted negative nasty comments and emojis after that had some bites and then all of them left .

Next day Almee came and confronted Marzin about all crap that he had written on the picture posted she, was fuming and then he replied,

You deserve it who names there dog biscuit I wonder people will one day eat him after getting to know you named him biscuit and gosh

So ,much make up on your face why you applied it looking like a whole make -up shop anything else R you done she asked and yes,

He replied listen this behavior of yours change it one day you will land up in big trouble oh god iam scared someone save me and laughed.

While holding on to his stomach and left the corridors of the campus..

And falling into this treacherous trap of being cool he would troll and post negative comments cn Friends Book on the pictures of.

Other peoples profiles that would be mean and savage and when his classmates would warn would smile. and make comments on them making them feel dumb in front of him,

This habit of posting on social media started becoming an addiction that he started bunking lectures attendance was just a dot,

Would lie about going to college and would go sit in the park then visit the mall shop and click pictures, post stories to prove that,

Yes life is a happening one and that day as he came back and was posting stories came across a picture of a couple in the same mall,

The girlfriend was wearing a black dress and her boyfriend proposed to her while sitting cn one knee and a, rose in hand the girl had,

Huge spectacles and a burnt scar under the eye however as we say some love stories are beyond looks and beauty so MR cool decided,

To give the boy a piece of his mind and posted a huge essay filled with comments that can cause any, persons blood to boil.

The girlfriend was reading those comments while her boyfriend was on a call soon reading that essay cried, her heart out and soon,

He came and asked what happened may be her parents have an objection with our relationship she showed the comments to him,

On the phone and his essay irked him to the core what does he think of himself will not spare him were his words,

She sensed something dangerous is going to happen witnessing the anger in his eyes held the hand of her, man and said see relax just,

Leave it and lets focus on our future and he replied no dear who the hell he is so much negativity and is, giving gyaan when not asked for.

He shall be punished let me drop you home first she requested him but was adamant to teach MR cool a lesson so made another id on.

Friends book and sent him a friend request saw the name Grossiya and accepted the request instantly and, then on all stories posted,

Would post comments full of compliments and praise he also got hold of his phone number which was. posted on official page and.

Then would call in the middle of the night by first saying hey love you and then other call would be come. meet me or I will die and the blame of my death will be on you why a bright future of yours should be in dark because of refusing to ,meet someone who likes you like anything in this world.

Soon these calls would be received all day and then felt petrified thought to go and meet this girl and sort, out the matter,

As he reached the place saw a group of guys approaching him and one of them replied Hi Marzin Iam. Grossiya your lover and those guys had chains , sticks and wrist bands with spikes and then things ,

Were clear that it was a trap being laid tried to run they got hold of him and removed his clothes and, clicked pictures and said,

You trolled my girlfriend thinking nothing will happen now be ready to face the consequences the glasses, he wore and phone was lost unable,

Find it and soon went back home opened the page on the laptop saw pics uploaded on social media couldn't, take it and lost,

His senses kept screaming social media is alive social media is alive iam dead iam dead his parents saw and got a doctor immediately,

The doctor said he needs counselling and therapy was suspended from college for not submitting any tutorial and no attendance,

The bright future became dark as one could imagine in the wake of being the coolest guy he forgot to, differentiate between what is right and

What is wrong what is ethical and what is unethical we all have to beat consequences of our actions some day or the other.

So social media should be used very wisely and be careful what you post ,as well as comments being, written on anyones pictures dont try and be oversmart thinking nothing is going to happen what you,

have sown is what you reap.